Penguin Readers

MOOMIN AND THE HAT

ADAPTED FROM
FINN FAMILY MOOMINTROLL

TOVE JANSSON

LEVEL

3

RETOLD BY DULCIE FRY
ILLUSTRATED BY TOVE JANSSON
SERIES EDITOR: SORREL PITTS

PENGUIN BOOKS

UK | USA | Canada | Ireland | Australia
India | New Zealand | South Africa

Penguin Books is part of the Penguin Random House group of companies
whose addresses can be found at global.penguinrandomhouse.com.
www.penguin.co.uk www.puffin.co.uk www.ladybird.co.uk

Penguin
Random House
UK

Moomin and the Hat adapted from *Finn Family Moomintroll*
First published in Finland as *Trollkarlens Hatt* 1948
Translation published in English by Ernest Benn Ltd 1950
Published by Puffin Books 1961, 2019
This Penguin Readers edition published by Penguin Books Ltd, 2024
001

Original text written by Tove Jansson
Text for Penguin Readers edition adapted by Dulcie Fry
Characters and artwork are the original creation of Tove Jansson
Copyright © Moomin Characters™, 2024
Design project management by Dynamo Limited

The moral right of the original author and illustrator has been asserted

Printed and bound in Great Britain by Clays Ltd, Elcograf S.p.A.

The authorized representative in the EEA is Penguin Random House Ireland,
Morrison Chambers, 32 Nassau Street, Dublin D02 YH68.

A CIP catalogue record for this book is available from the British Library

ISBN: 978–0–241–63680–0

All correspondence to:
Penguin Books
Penguin Random House Children's
One Embassy Gardens, 8 Viaduct Gardens,
London SW11 7BW

Contents

People in the story

Moomintroll

Moominmamma and
Moominpappa

Sniff

Snufkin

Snorkmaiden

The Hemulen

Thingumy and Bob

New words

cave

handbag

mouth-organ

pancakes

ruby

valley

Note about the story

Tove Jansson was born in Finland in 1914. She was an artist and she also wrote many books for adults and children. She drew her first Moomin in the 1930s for fun, and in 1945 she wrote her first Moomin book. Tove became famous all over the world for her Moomin stories. She wrote nine books about the Moomin family and their friends, and drew all the pictures for them.

Tove lived and worked in the city of Helsinki in the winter, and every summer she stayed near the sea for a few months. The seasons – winter, spring, summer and autumn – are an important part of *Moomin and the Hat*. The winter is long and dark in Finland while the summer nights are very light.

Tove Jansson died in 2001 at the age of 86.

Before-reading questions

1 Look at the cover of the book. What do you think will happen in the story?

2 Look at the "People in the story" on page 6. What are they like, do you think?

3 Read the "Note about the story" and look quickly at the pictures in the book. What is it like in the Moomins' world, do you think?

4 Look again at the pictures in the book. Find:
  a a river
  b a mountain
  c the moon.

CHAPTER ONE
The hat

One grey morning, the first snow began to fall in the **Valley*** of the Moomins. It fell softly and quietly, and in a few hours everything was white.

Moomintroll stood outside his house and watched the snow. "Tonight," he thought, "we'll go to bed and sleep all through the winter."

All moomintrolls go to sleep about November. This is a good idea if you do not like the cold and the long, dark winter.

"The snow has come!" Moomintroll said to his mother.

"I know," said Moominmamma. "I've made all our beds."

The Moomin family and all their friends had a small meal. Then, they said goodnight and went to bed. The snow fell more heavily and nearly **covered** Moominhouse. The clocks stopped. Winter was here.

---

*Definitions of words in **bold** can be found in the glossary on pages 93–95.

The first bird of spring arrived in Moominvalley at four o'clock in the morning. He sang his little song and then he flew away to the east.

Moomintroll woke up and lay in his bed for a long time.

"Where am I?" he thought. "Oh, I remember!" Moomintroll still felt tired and he tried to go back to sleep. But then he saw that Snufkin's bed was empty and that his hat was not there.

"Where is Snufkin?" he thought. He went to the window and looked down. He could see the **rope ladder**. "Oh! Snufkin has gone out of the window."

He climbed out of the window and went down the rope ladder. He stood at the bottom and listened. He could hear music. Snufkin was playing his happiest song on his **mouth-organ**. Moomintroll began running towards the music.

Snufkin was sitting on the bridge over the river.

"Hello," said Moomintroll, sitting down next to him.

"Hello to you," said Snufkin and he started playing his mouth-organ again.

They sat there for a while, feeling happy. They could remember many strange adventures on this river and meeting lots of new friends there. Moomintroll's mother and father were always happy for these friends to come and stay. Because of this, Moominhouse was quite full. But it was a very happy house. Strange and surprising things often happened there, and nobody was ever bored.

Snufkin finished his song and put his mouth-organ in his **pocket**.

"Is Sniff still sleeping?" he asked.

"Yes," said Moomintroll. "He always sleeps a week longer than the others."

"Then we must wake him up," said Snufkin and he jumped down. "We must do something special today because the weather is going to be nice."

They stood under Sniff's window and Moomintroll **whistled**. Three short **whistles** first and then a long one through his **paws**. This meant, "Something is happening."

Nothing moved above, so Moomintroll whistled again. This time, he did it more loudly.

"I'm sleeping!" shouted Sniff, angrily.

"Come down and don't be angry," said Snufkin. "We're going to do something special today."

Sniff got out of bed and climbed down his rope ladder. Moomintroll, Snufkin and Sniff began to walk up the hill. Everywhere, lots of small **creatures** were waking up after the long winter. Many of them were getting their houses ready for spring.

"Happy spring!" said a little **mouse**. "And how was the winter with you?"

"Very nice, thank you," said Moomintroll. "Did you sleep well?"

"Fine," said the mouse. "Please say hello to your father and mother for me."

Moomintroll, Snufkin and Sniff kept walking up the hill. They met more people and stopped to talk to a lot of them. But higher up the hill, they saw fewer people. And near the top of the hill, there were only one or two **mice**.

It was wet everywhere.

"Ugh, horrible!" said Moomintroll. "Snow is never good for a Moomin."

"Listen, Moomintroll," said Snufkin. "I have an idea. Let's go to the top of the mountain and make a pile of stones. We can show that we are the first ones there."

"Yes, let's go," said Sniff and he started to walk quickly because he wanted to get there before Moomintroll and Snufkin.

When they got to the top of the mountain, they could feel the March wind around them. In the west, they could see the sea. In the east, they could see the river and more mountains. In the north, they could see the great forest.

In the south, they could see the Moominhouse **roof** and smoke, and they knew that Moominmamma was cooking breakfast. But Sniff did not see any of these things because a hat lay on the top of the mountain. A tall, black hat.

"Someone got here first!" Sniff said.

Moomintroll looked at the hat. "It's a very special hat," he said. "You should wear it, Snufkin!"

"No, no," said Snufkin because he loved his old green hat. "It's much too new."

"Father might like it," said Moomintroll.

"Well, let's take it home with us," said Sniff. "I'm very hungry and it's time for breakfast."

And the three friends went home with the Hobgoblin's Hat. It was a **magic** hat, but the three friends did not know that yet.

CHAPTER TWO

The clouds

Moomintroll, Snufkin and Sniff arrived back at Moominhouse. Moominmamma was in the kitchen making breakfast, and Moominpappa was in the sitting room.

"We've found a hat," said Moomintroll. "Look! It's a beautiful new hat for you!"

Moominpappa looked at the hat closely. Then he put it on his head and looked in the mirror. The hat was too big for him and it nearly covered his eyes. He looked quite strange.

"Mother!" shouted Moomintroll. "Come and look at Father!"

Moominmamma opened the kitchen door and looked at Moominpappa.

"How do I look?" asked Moominpappa.

"You look very handsome in it, but it's a bit too big," said Moominmamma. "And I think that you look better without a hat."

Moominpappa looked in the mirror again and then he put the hat on the table.

"You're right," he said. "Some people look better without hats."

"Of course, dear," said Moominmamma, kindly. "Now eat your eggs, children. You must be hungry after the winter."

"But what shall we do with the hat?" asked Sniff.

"It can be a **bin**," said Moominpappa and he went upstairs.

Snufkin smiled. "Why do people need so many things?" he thought. Snufkin only had his clothes and his mouth-organ, but that was enough.

Snufkin put the hat down on the floor between the table and the kitchen door. The three friends ate their breakfast, then Moomintroll said, "Let's go and see Snorkmaiden." He threw his **eggshell** into the bin and they went out into the garden.

The dining room was now empty. The Hobgoblin's Hat stood in the corner between the table and the kitchen door. Moomintroll's eggshell lay in the bottom of the hat. And then something really strange happened. The eggshell began to change.

Why was this happening? Well, if something lies in the Hobgoblin's Hat, it begins to change into something quite different. It was lucky for Moominpappa that the hat was too big and that he did not wear it for long!

The eggshell became soft and it started to get bigger and bigger. After some time, it filled the hat. Then, four small clouds **floated** out of the hat. They floated out of the house, down the steps and into the garden. Then, they stayed just above the ground. The hat was empty.

"Oh!" said Moomintroll.

"Is there a fire in the house?" asked Snorkmaiden. She looked worried.

The clouds floated in front of them and waited. Snorkmaiden touched one with her paw.

"It's very soft," she said.

The others came nearer and felt it, too. Snufkin slowly pushed one of the clouds. It floated away for a bit and then stopped again.

"Where did they come from?" asked Sniff.

"I don't know. It's very strange," said Moomintroll. "Shall we get Mother?"

"No, no," said Snorkmaiden. "Let's play with them first."

And she pulled a cloud to her and jumped on to it. She floated up and down on the cloud, laughing loudly.

"Can I have one, too?" asked Sniff, jumping on to another cloud. The cloud did a little jump over the ground.

"Wow!" Sniff cried. "It moved!"

They all jumped on to the clouds and shouted happily. Sniff discovered that he could move his cloud in different directions with his feet. He could turn left and right, and he could also go up and down.

They had a fun time playing with the clouds. They floated up to the tops of the trees and to the top of Moominhouse. Moomintroll floated outside Moominpappa's window and shouted, "Hello!"

Moominpappa ran to his window. "Oh!" he shouted. "What is happening?"

Next, Moomintroll floated to the kitchen window and shouted to his mother.

"What have you found now, dear?" she said. "Don't fall down!"

"Let's fly somewhere on our clouds," Moomintroll said to Snorkmaiden.

"Yes!" she said. "Where shall we go?"

"Let's go and see the Hemulen and give him a surprise," said Moomintroll.

The Hemulen was not in the garden, so Moomintroll and Snorkmaiden floated into the forest to look for him. After a while, they saw him. He was walking along with his hands behind his back and his eyes on the ground. Moomintroll and Snorkmaiden flew down and stopped next to him.

"Good morning!" they called.

"Oh!" shouted the Hemulen. "Don't jump at me suddenly like that!"

"Oh, sorry," said Snorkmaiden. "But look at us! We're riding on little clouds!"

"That is very strange," said the Hemulen. "But then you often do strange things so I'm not very surprised. Anyway, I'm feeling quite sad right now."

"Why?" asked Snorkmaiden.

"Have you lost a special stamp again?" asked Moomintroll.

"No," said the Hemulen. "I have all my stamps. That is the problem. There are no more stamps to add to my **collection**. I've finished it."

"Isn't that a good thing?" said Snorkmaiden.

"No!" said the Hemulen. "Because what do I do now?"

"Oh, I think that I'm beginning to understand," said Moomintroll, slowly. "**Collecting** things is more fun than just owning them."

"Dear Hemulen," said Snorkmaiden. "I have an idea. Can you start collecting something different? Something new?"

"That's a good idea," said the Hemulen, but he still looked worried. He did not want to look too happy so soon after being so sad.

"**Butterflies**?" asked Moomintroll.

"No," said the Hemulen and he looked sad again. "My second cousin collects butterflies, and I hate him."

"**Shells**?" said Snorkmaiden.

"No," said the Hemulen, sadly.

"Well, then I really don't know," said Snorkmaiden.

"We'll think of something," said Moomintroll. "I'm sure that Mother will have some ideas."

The Hemulen walked away and Moomintroll and Snorkmaiden rode their clouds to the top of the trees. It was sunny up there. They thought more about the problem of the Hemulen's new collection. But they did not have many more ideas. It was warm now, and they lay on their backs, feeling tired.

Suddenly, they saw a butterfly. In spring in Moominvalley, if the first butterfly you see is yellow, you will have a happy summer. If it is white, you will have a quiet summer. Nobody talks about black and brown butterflies because they are much too sad.

"Look! A butterfly!" said Snorkmaiden. "What colour is it?"

"It's **gold**!" said Moomintroll. "I've never seen a gold butterfly before. What does that mean?"

"Gold is even better than yellow," said Snorkmaiden.

Later, when they got home for dinner, they met the Hemulen at the house. He looked very happy.

"What is it?" asked Moomintroll.

"I've decided to become a *botanist*! I'm going to collect and study plants," shouted the Hemulen. "Look!"

He showed them a small plant with yellow flowers.

"It's a *Gagea lutea*," he said. "This will be number one in my collection. It's beautiful."

The Hemulen put the plant on the table.

"Put it in the corner, Hemulen dear," said Moominmamma, "I want to put the soup there." Then, she filled everyone's plate with soup. "Now, has everyone had a good time today?" she asked.

"We've had a wonderful time!" they all cried.

Next morning, Moomintroll looked for the clouds, but he could not find them anywhere. The eggshell was back in the bottom of the Hobgoblin's Hat. And still nobody knew that the hat was a magic hat.

CHAPTER THREE
Moomintroll changes

It was a warm summer day, and it was raining in Moominvalley. Moomintroll and his friends decided to play a game inside.

Sniff stood in the corner with his nose in his paws and counted to ten. Everybody **hid**. Then Sniff turned round and started to look for the others. Moomintroll hid under a table, but he knew that it was not a good place to **hide**.

"I'm sure that Sniff will look here," he thought.

Then, Moomintroll saw the tall, black hat in the corner and he had an idea! He quickly got out from under the table and pulled the hat over his head. It only covered the top half of his body so he pulled his **tail** inside the hat and tried to be small.

"Sniff will never find me now!" he thought, and laughed. He heard Sniff find the others. Now, they were all looking for Moomintroll. Moomintroll waited for a short time and then he took the hat off.

"I'm here! Look at me!" he said.

Sniff was quiet for a long time. Then he said, "I don't want to look at you."

The others said nothing.

Oh dear! Moomintroll did not look like Moomintroll any more. The fat parts of his body were now thin, and the small parts were big. He had very long, thin legs and he looked very different. But Moomintroll did not know this.

"Are you all very surprised?" he said. "I found a very good place to hide."

"We *are* surprised," said Sniff. "But only because you're very ugly."

"You're very unkind," said Moomintroll, sadly. "Did you get tired looking for me? What do you want to do now?"

"First, maybe, you should tell us your name," said Snorkmaiden.

Moomintroll thought that this was a new game. So, he laughed and said, "I'm the King of California!"

"And I'm Snorkmaiden," said Snorkmaiden.

"I'm called Sniff," said Sniff.

"I'm Snufkin," said Snufkin.

"Oh dear! You're all very boring," said Moomintroll. "Those are not new names. Now let's go out. I think that it's stopped raining." And he went down the steps into the garden. The others followed him.

"Who's that?" asked the Hemulen. He was in the garden, looking at flowers.

"It's the King of California, I think," said Snorkmaiden.

"Is he going to live here?" asked the Hemulen.

"Moomintroll will decide that," said Sniff. "But we're still looking for him. We can't find him."

Moomintroll laughed.

"You can be very funny sometimes," he said. "Well, let's go and look for Moomintroll."

"Do you know him?" asked Snufkin.

"Ye-es," said Moomintroll. "I know him very well!"

He was really enjoying this new game. He thought that it was very funny and he was very good at it.

"How do you know Moomintroll?" asked Snorkmaiden.

"We were born at the same time," said Moomintroll, laughing. "But he's very naughty, you know!"

"Don't talk about Moomintroll like that!" said Snorkmaiden, angrily. "He's the best Moomin in the world."

"Is that true?" he said. "Well, I think that he's a terrible Moomin."

When she heard this, Snorkmaiden began to cry.

"Go away," said Sniff. "Or we'll have to sit on your head."

"All right, all right," Moomintroll said. "It's only a game. But I'm very happy that you think that I'm the best Moomin in the world."

"But we don't!" shouted Sniff. "Take away this ugly king. He says terrible things about our Moomintroll."

And Sniff and Snufkin jumped on top of Moomintroll. He was too surprised and could not stop them. Then, Moominmamma came out of the house.

"What are you doing there, children?" she cried. "Stop fighting!"

"Mother!" Moomintroll cried. "They started it. It wasn't me. There are two of them and I'm only one."

"Yes, that is true," said Moominmamma. "But who are you, my little creature?"

"Oh, please stop this terrible game," cried Moomintroll. "It isn't funny any more. I am Moomintroll, and you are my mother. And that is all!"

"You aren't Moomintroll," said Snorkmaiden. "He has beautiful little ears, but yours are huge!"

Moomintroll felt his ears. They *were* huge. This was very strange!

"But I *am* Moomintroll!" he cried. "It is me!"

"Moomintroll has a nice little tail, but yours is huge, like a big brush," said Sniff.

And, oh dear, it was true! Moomintroll felt behind him with his paw.

"And your eyes are like soup plates," said Snufkin. "Moomintroll's eyes are small and kind!"

"Doesn't anyone know that this is me?" Moomintroll asked. "Look at me, Mother. You must know your own Moomintroll."

Moominmamma looked at him. She looked into his frightened eyes for a very long time, and then she said, quietly, "Yes, you are my Moomintroll."

And then he began to change. His ears, eyes and tail got smaller, and his nose and stomach grew. He looked like Moomintroll again.

"It's all right now, my dear," said Moominmamma. "I will always know you."

CHAPTER FOUR
Berry juice

Later, Sniff asked Moomintroll, "How did you change? What did you do?"

"I don't know," said Moomintroll. "I didn't do anything and I didn't say any dangerous words. I just hid under that hat – it's a bin now."

"You hid under the *hat*?" asked Sniff.

"Y-yes," said Moomintroll, and they both thought for a long time.

Suddenly, they shouted, "The hat is magic!"

"We should tell the others!" said Moomintroll. They found Moominpappa and Moominmamma and told them about the hat.

"That hat is very dangerous," said Moominpappa. "We must throw it in the river."

So, the Moomin family and their friends took the hat and threw it in the river. They watched it float away.

"Goodbye, magic hat," said Moominmamma.

"The clouds were fun," said Moomintroll, sadly. "I didn't like changing into that strange creature but I liked the clouds."

———

That night, Moomintroll could not sleep. He lay in his bed and looked out at the light June night. Sometimes, he could hear the noises of small creatures outside and the air was sweet with the smell of flowers.

Snufkin was not back yet. On nights like this, he liked to go for walks and play his mouth-organ. But Moomintroll could not hear his songs and he felt sad. In the summer, Snufkin often slept outside. Maybe he was looking for a place to sleep? Suddenly, Moomintroll heard a whistle. He knew that the whistle meant, "Secrets!" He stopped feeling sad and went to the window. Snufkin was waiting under the rope ladder. Moomintroll climbed down feeling excited.

"Can you keep a secret?" Snufkin asked.

"Yes!" said Moomintroll.

"The hat floated down the river, but it's stopped on a **sandbank**. Do you want to see it?"

"Yes!" said Moomintroll again, and the two friends walked down to the river.

"The hat is doing magic things again. Look! The river water is turning red," said Snufkin. "I think that we should go and get the hat because lots of creatures live in the river. They will be very frightened if they see this terrible water."

"Yes, you're right!" said Moomintroll.

"The hat is over there," Snufkin said. "Look at the dark water. Can you see?"

"Not really," said Moomintroll. "I can't see at night like you."

"How are we going to get the hat?" said Snufkin, looking at the river.

"I can swim quite well if the water isn't too cold," said Moomintroll.

"Are you sure?" asked Snufkin.

"Yes, of course!" replied Moomintroll.

"Don't put your foot in the hat," said Snufkin. "Hold it with your paw."

Moomintroll got into the warm summer water and started swimming. The river was fast and he felt a bit frightened. Then, he saw the sandbank and there was something black on it. He swam closer and soon he felt **sand** under his feet. He stood up on the sandbank. Dark water was coming out of the hat and into the river. Moomintroll touched the dark water with his paw and then put it in his mouth.

"Oh!" he said. "It's **berry** juice!"

"Have you got the hat?" shouted Snufkin.

"Oh, yes!" Moomintroll shouted. And he swam across the river with his tail round the hat. But it was difficult swimming with a heavy hat behind him and, when he arrived back, he was quite tired.

"Here it is," he said.

"Fine!" said Snufkin. "But what should we do with it?"

"Well, I think that we should keep it," said Moomintroll. "It makes berry juice. Think about it. We can have berry juice all the time! And maybe we will see those little clouds again, too."

So, they decided to take the hat home. Snufkin carried the hat and Moomintroll followed him. But, suddenly, Snufkin stopped.

"What is it?" asked Moomintroll.

"I can see birds!" cried Snufkin. "There are three little yellow birds on the bridge, but it is the middle of the night. How strange!"

"I'm not a bird," said the nearest one. "I'm a fish!"

"Yes! We are fishes, all three of us!" said his friend.

"It's that hat again," said Snufkin. "I'm sure that those three little fishes were swimming in it. The hat has changed them. Let's go! We must find a safe place for it at home."

Moomintroll stayed close behind Snufkin while they walked through the forest. He could hear noises and sometimes he could see small eyes behind the trees.

"It's a beautiful night!" said a voice behind them.

"Yes, it is," Moomintroll replied and he felt a bit frightened when a small creature went past him.

It was starting to get lighter. There was a light blue **glow** over the sea and the sky. Morning was here.

Snufkin and Moomintroll carried the Hobgoblin's Hat home.

CHAPTER FIVE
The cave

It was nearly the end of July, and it was very hot in Moominvalley. The trees looked tired and the river was thin and brown. Moomintroll and his friends felt tired and hot.

"Mother!" said Moomintroll. "We don't like this weather. Find us something to do!"

"Can you go to the **cave** for a few days?" said Moominmamma. "It's cooler there by the sea and you can swim all day."

"Can we sleep in the cave, too?" Moomintroll asked, excitedly.

"Of course," said Moominmamma. "I'll get some food ready for you. You can take some **pancakes**."

So, Moomintroll, Snufkin, Sniff, Snorkmaiden and the Hemulen went to the cave. It was very exciting to stay there. They put a lamp in the middle of the floor, and they made beds in the sand. They ate some of their pancakes and Snufkin played his mouth-organ. Everyone felt happy. The red glow from the sun filled the cave for a while and then it started to get dark.

"Shall I tell you a terrible story?" Snufkin asked.

"Is it very terrible?" asked the Hemulen.

"It's quite terrible," said Snufkin.

"OK, you can tell your story," said the Hemulen, "but I'll tell you when I get frightened."

"Good," said Snufkin. "It's a strange story. A bird told it to me. Well, there is a very high mountain at the end of the world. It is very black and you can't see the bottom of it. You can only see clouds. But there is a house at the very top of the mountain. It is the Hobgoblin's House, and it looks like this."

Snufkin drew a house in the sand.

"Hasn't it got any windows?" asked Sniff.

"No," said Snufkin, "and it hasn't got a door or a roof. The Hobgoblin rides on a big black cat called a **panther**. Every night, they fly out and collect **rubies** in the Hobgoblin's Hat."

"Rubies!" asked Sniff. "Where does he get them from?"

"The Hobgoblin can change into anything," replied Snufkin, "and then he can go anywhere to find rubies. He can go under the ground and even to the bottom of the sea."

"What does the Hobgoblin do with all these rubies?" asked Sniff.

"He doesn't do anything with them. He just collects them, like the Hemulen collects plants," said Snufkin.

"What did you say?" asked the Hemulen.

"The Hobgoblin has a house full of rubies," said Snufkin. "There are piles of them everywhere. He has put some of the rubies in the walls and they look like the eyes of wild creatures. The Hobgoblin's eyes are red, too, and they **glow** in the dark!"

"Now I'm nearly frightened," said the Hemulen.

"This Hobgoblin is very lucky to have a house full of rubies," said Sniff.

"Well, he isn't very happy," said Snufkin. "And he won't be happy until he finds the King's **Ruby**. That ruby is nearly as big as the black panther's head and it glows like fire. The Hobgoblin has looked everywhere for it but he hasn't found it. He's on the moon looking for it now."

"But is all this true?" asked Sniff.

"Maybe," said Snufkin. "But the bird told me more. She thinks that the Hobgoblin had a tall, black hat. He lost it a few months ago."

"No!" cried Moomintroll.

The others made excited noises.

"What's that?" asked the Hemulen. "What are you talking about?"

"The hat," Sniff told him. "Do you remember the tall, black hat? I found it on top of the mountain in the spring. It's the Hobgoblin's Hat!"

"Oh no! But he might come to Moominvalley to look for his hat!" said Snorkmaiden. "Where is it now?"

"It's on the table under the mirror and nobody thinks about it much now," said Moomintroll. "We must talk to Mother about this. Snufkin, is it a long way to the moon?"

"Yes, it is quite a long way," replied Snufkin. "And I'm sure that it will take a long time for the Hobgoblin to look everywhere on the moon."

Everyone was quiet. They were all thinking about the black hat on the table under the mirror at home. Suddenly, the Hemulen jumped and said, "Did you hear that? There's something outside."

They all listened. Was it the Hobgoblin's black panther?

"It's only rain," said Moomintroll. "It has come after many weeks. Let's go to sleep."

And they got into their beds and went to sleep.

In the morning, the Hemulen woke up suddenly. Rain was coming in through the roof of the cave and his bed was wet.

"Oh no!" he cried. "Yesterday was too hot and now it's too wet."

Soon, the others woke up. They were cold and wet so they decided to go home. The rain got worse on their way back and they could not see very well. After some time, they arrived back in the garden.

Suddenly, Snorkmaiden stopped. "We've come the wrong way!" she said.

"No, we haven't," said Moomintroll. "Look, there's the bridge and this is our garden."

"Yes, but where's the house?" asked Snorkmaiden.

It was very strange. Moominhouse was not there.

CHAPTER SIX

The jungle

Let's go back to the Moomintroll house earlier that day.

Moominmamma was happy that it was raining.

"Now everything in the garden will grow!" she said. "And the family are safe and dry in the cave!"

She decided to make the house tidier. She started collecting clothes, Moomintroll's strange stones, bits of wood, and other things. She found some of the Hemulen's plants on top of the radio. Without thinking, she put the plants in the Hobgoblin's Hat.

Then Moominmamma went upstairs to her room and lay on her bed, listening to the rain on the roof. Soon, she went to sleep.

Then something very strange started happening downstairs. The Hemulen's plants were growing slowly out of the hat. Then they grew up the walls, through doors, and up the stairs. Flowers and fruits started growing, too, and the house was full of quiet noises. Sometimes, a fruit fell on to the **carpet**. The noises woke Moominmamma up but she thought that it was only the rain. She went to sleep again.

Moominpappa was writing his life story in his room upstairs. Suddenly, a blue fruit fell on to his paper.

"Oh! Moomintroll and Sniff must be home again!" he said, and he turned to look behind him.

But it was not a person – it was a thick **bush**. It was full of yellow berries. Next, small blue fruits started falling all around him. There was a huge **branch** growing slowly near the window. Smaller branches were growing from the branch in all directions.

"Hello!" shouted Moominpappa. "Wake up, everybody! Come quickly!"

Moominmamma woke up and she saw that her room was full of small, white flowers.

"Oh, how beautiful!" she said. "Moomintroll has done this for me for a surprise."

"Hello!" shouted Moominpappa again. "Open the door! I can't get out!"

But Moominmamma could not open the door because there were too many plants. She looked around. There was a small forest on the stairs, and the living room was like a **jungle**.

"Oh!" said Moominmamma. "Of course, it's that hat again."

The plants grew up through the house and out on to the roof. Soon, they covered all of Moominhouse with a thick, green carpet.

———

Moomintroll stood and looked at the green jungle outside Moominhouse. Flowers were opening and fruits were turning from green to yellow, and from yellow to red.

"The house *was* here," said Sniff.

"It still is. It's inside that jungle," said Moomintroll. "But we can't get in and Pappa and Mamma can't get out."

"This is more hat **magic**," thought Snufkin. "It's beginning to get silly."

"Look!" shouted Sniff. "The **cellar** door is open!"

"Come quickly!" said Moomintroll. "Let's go in that way."

Moomintroll, Sniff, Snufkin and Snorkmaiden all climbed down into the dark cellar. The Hemulen came last.

"The door is too small," he shouted. "I can't get in!"

"Stay outside," said Moomintroll. "You can study the plants on the house!"

So, the Hemulen stayed outside in the rain and Moomintroll and the others got into the house through the cellar. They could hear loud noises upstairs. Then, there was a cry. Moominpappa was out of his room!

"Mamma! Pappa!" shouted Moomintroll, going up the cellar stairs. He was happy to see that the door to the house was open. "What has happened?" he cried. "Why is there a jungle here?"

"Well, dear," replied Moominmamma, "I think that it must be because of the Hobgoblin's Hat again. But come up here! I've found a berry bush in the cupboard."

After that, the children played games in the jungle all afternoon. Everybody had a wonderful

time. They forgot about the Hemulen outside in the rain. He was now very wet.

When evening arrived, it stopped raining. At the same time, something strange started happening to the jungle. It started getting smaller. The fruit fell to the ground and the flowers died. In the garden, the Hemulen watched for a while, and then he pulled at a branch. It was very dry and the Hemulen had an idea. He collected a huge pile of branches and made a fire in the middle of the garden. He sat next to it and soon felt warmer.

Then the Moomin family and their friends pushed their way out of the house into the garden. They saw the happy and warm Hemulen next to the fire.

"Let's put the jungle on the fire," said Moominpappa.

And they took all the bits of jungle from the house and threw them on the fire. The fire became huge and everyone in Moominvalley could see it.

CHAPTER SEVEN
Thingumy and Bob

Early one morning at the beginning of August, Thingumy and Bob arrived in Moominvalley. Thingumy wore a red hat and Bob carried a huge **suitcase**. Their journey was long and they were tired. They rested for a while near the top of the mountain and looked down over the valley. They could see Moominhouse and smoke.

"Smoke," said Thingumy. "I'm hungry."

"*Foke* means *smood*," said Bob.

And they walked down the mountain, talking in their strange language until they arrived at the Moominhouse. Just then, Moominmamma opened the window and shouted, "Coffee!"

This frightened Thingumy and Bob and they jumped through the open doors of the potato cellar.

"Oh!" said Moominmamma. "I think that two mice just ran into the cellar. Sniff, take them some milk."

Then she saw Thingumy and Bob's suitcase.

"Oh, they've brought a suitcase. I think that they want to stay," thought Moominmamma.

"Moominpappa!" she shouted. "Please make two more very, very small beds."

Thingumy and Bob stayed in the cellar and hid in a pile of potatoes.

"I can *fell smood*," said Thingumy. "I'm hungry."

"Quiet! Someone's coming," said Bob.

Then the cellar door opened and Sniff stood at the top of the stairs. He had a lamp in one paw and a small plate of milk in his other paw.

"Hi! Where are you?" he shouted. "Do you want some milk?"

Thingumy and Bob did not say anything.

"I'm not going to stand here all day!" said Sniff, angrily. "Silly old mice!"

Thingumy and Bob did not like this. "You're a *milly* old *souse*!" they replied.

"Oh! They speak a foreign language," thought Sniff. "I will tell Moominmamma."

He **locked** the cellar door and ran into the kitchen.

"Well? Did they like the milk?" asked Moominmamma.

"They talk in a foreign language," said Sniff. "I can't understand them."

"What's the language like?" asked Moomintroll.

"'You're a *milly* old *souse!*'" said Sniff.

"Oh. This is going to be difficult. How will I ask them anything?" said Moominmamma.

"We'll soon learn their language," said Moomintroll. "It sounds easy."

"I think that I understand it," said the Hemulen. "*Milly* old *souse* means silly old mouse. I don't think that they like Sniff."

Sniff's face went red.

"Well, if you're that clever you can go and talk to them," he said.

So, the Hemulen went to the top of the cellar stairs.

"Welcome to *Hoominmouse!*" he cried, in a kind voice.

Thingumy and Bob looked up from the potato pile.

"*Mere's* some *hilk*," said the Hemulen, and he showed them the small plate of milk.

51

Thingumy and Bob ran up the cellar stairs and into the living room. Sniff looked at them. They were much smaller than he was and he felt kinder.

"Hello," he said, very slowly like they were small children. "It's nice to meet you."

"Thanks. It's *mice* to *neet* you, too," said Thingumy.

"Did I *fell smood*?" asked Bob.

"What are they saying now?" asked Moominmamma.

"They can smell food. They're hungry," said the Hemulen. "But I still don't think that they like Sniff very much."

Sniff's face went red again and he walked angrily out of the room.

"*Won't dorry* about him. He's often like that," said the Hemulen.

"Come and have some coffee," said Moominmamma and she took Thingumy and Bob into the kitchen.

Thingumy and Bob decided to stay at Moominhouse. They did not make much noise. Most of the time they held hands, and they always kept their suitcase with them. But, when the evening arrived on their first day, they got very worried. They ran up and down the stairs many times and then they hid under the living room carpet.

"What's the matter with them?" asked Moominmamma.

"*Mot's* the *watter*?" the Hemulen asked.

"The Groke is coming!" said Bob.

"Groke? Who's that?" asked the Hemulen, feeling a bit frightened.

"She's *tig* and *berrible*!" said Bob. "Lock all the doors!"

The Hemulen ran to Moominmamma and told her the terrible news.

"A big and terrible Groke is coming here," he said. "We must lock all the doors tonight."

"Oh dear," said Moominmamma. "But I don't think that we have any keys. We only have a key for the cellar."

She went to talk to Moominpappa.

"We must get ready," said Moominpappa. "A large Groke might be dangerous. I will put an **alarm clock** in the living room. If anyone comes into the house, it will start ringing. Now, go and find things to fight with. Thingumy and Bob can sleep under my bed."

But Thingumy and Bob were already hiding in a cupboard. Moominpappa went into the garden to get his gun. It was getting dark outside and the wind was **blowing** through the trees.

"Maybe the Groke is hiding behind a bush," he thought and he walked more quickly.

"We must leave the light on all night," he said when he arrived back in the house. He pushed the sofa in front of the door. "And Snufkin, you must sleep in the house tonight. Now, let's go to bed."

It was very exciting. There was a lot of noise from everyone while they went to their rooms. Then everything became quiet.

It was midnight. Then it was one o'clock. At two o'clock, Sniff woke up feeling hungry. He got out of bed and went downstairs. But he forgot about the alarm clock and walked straight past it. The alarm clock started ringing very loudly. Everybody woke up and ran downstairs with stones, **spades** and knives.

"Where's the Groke?" asked Moomintroll.

"Oh, it was only me," said Sniff. "I was hungry. I forgot about Thingumy and Bob's silly Groke."

Suddenly, the Hemulen said, "Quiet! Did you hear that? There's something outside."

"I'm sure that it's only a mouse," said Moomintroll. "I'll open the door and look."

Moomintroll pushed the sofa to the side and opened the door. And there was the Groke! She sat without moving at the bottom of the steps and looked at them with her big, round eyes.

The Groke was not very big and she did not look very dangerous. But they felt that she was very bad and that she could wait there forever. And *that* was terrible. Nobody did anything. The Groke sat there for a while and then she left.

But look! The ground was now **ice**!

Moominpappa closed the door.

"Hemulen!" he said. "Go and check that Thingumy and Bob are OK."

The Hemulen went to see Thingumy and Bob. He opened the cupboard door and looked in.

"Has she gone?" asked Thingumy.

"Yes, she's gone. It's OK. You can sleep again now," replied the Hemulen.

Thingumy and Bob pulled the suitcase nearer to them and went to sleep again.

"Can we go to bed again now?" asked Moominmamma.

"Yes, Mother," said Moomintroll. "Snufkin and I will stay downstairs."

Moomintroll and Snufkin sat in the living room until morning. But they did not see the Groke again that night.

CHAPTER EIGHT

The meeting

The next morning, the Hemulen went into the kitchen.

"Thingumy and Bob have told me more about the Groke," he said. "She wants their suitcase."

"That's terrible!" said Moominmamma.

"Yes, I know," said the Hemulen, "but, well, it *is* the Groke's suitcase."

"Oh," said Moominmamma. "That makes it more difficult then. Let's talk to Moomintroll. He'll have a good idea."

Moomintroll listened to them and then he said, "This is very interesting. We must have a **meeting**. Everyone should come to the garden at three o'clock to talk about this."

It was a warm afternoon and the garden looked beautiful with all the colours of late summer. Moomintroll was sitting in front of a box. He looked like a **judge**. Thingumy and Bob were sitting opposite him, eating **cherries**.

"I think that we should give the suitcase to the Groke," said Sniff.

"I don't agree," said the Hemulen. "You're only saying that because they called you a silly old mouse. I think that Thingumy and Bob should keep the suitcase."

"*I* will decide," said Moomintroll. "I am the judge. Now, let's begin the meeting."

He hit the box three times.

"Thingumy and Bob," said Moomintroll, "you can only say 'Yes' or 'No'. You can say nothing more. Is this suitcase yours or the Groke's?"

"Yes," said Thingumy.

"No," said Bob. He blew a cherry at the judge.

Then everyone started talking.

"Quiet!" said Moomintroll again. "Now I'm asking for the last time. Whose suitcase is it?"

"It's ours!" said Thingumy.

"Why do they say that?" asked the Hemulen. "Oh, I don't understand!"

Thingumy said something quietly in the Hemulen's ear.

"There is something inside the suitcase," said the Hemulen, "and this **Contents** is the Groke's."

"Ah!" said Sniff. "Well, we must give the Groke her Contents. Thingumy and Bob can keep their old suitcase."

"But *should* we give her the Contents?" asked the Hemulen. "The Groke is a terrible creature! Everyone can see that."

"She is terrible. That is true," replied Sniff. "But nobody likes her and she can't be very happy. She only has the Contents, and Thingumy and Bob have stolen them from her!" And he started to cry.

Moomintroll hit the box. "Quiet! Snorkmaiden, what do you think?" he cried.

"Well, I like Thingumy and Bob very much, and I've never liked the Groke," said Snorkmaiden.

"But right is right," said Moomintroll.

"Thingumy and Bob don't understand right and wrong, but we must do the right thing."

"But what *are* the Contents?" said Snorkmaiden. "Maybe we should look inside the suitcase. Then it will be easier to decide."

Thingumy said something in the Hemulen's ear.

"It's a secret," the Hemulen said. "Thingumy and Bob think that the Contents is the most beautiful thing in the world, but the Groke just thinks that it's the most expensive."

"This is difficult," said Moomintroll. "Thingumy and Bob were right to think that, but they were wrong to take the Contents. What should we do? I must think. Quiet now!"

Suddenly, a cold wind blew into the garden. The sun went behind a cloud and the colours in the garden did not look as bright as before.

"What was that?" asked Snufkin.

"She's here again," said Snorkmaiden, quietly.

The Groke sat in the grass and looked at them all angrily. Then she started moving nearer Thingumy and Bob.

"Help!" they shouted.

"Stop, Groke!" cried Moomintroll. "I have something to say to you."

The Groke stopped.

"I have decided," said Moomintroll. "I think that Thingumy and Bob should buy the Contents of the suitcase. Do you agree? What is your price?"

"High," said the Groke.

Then Moominmamma had an idea. She went into the house and came back with the Hobgoblin's Hat. She put the hat on the grass in front of the Groke.

"Here is the most special thing in Moominvalley, Groke!" said Moominmamma. "It is a magic hat. It can make berry juice and fruit trees. It can also make the most wonderful little clouds – you can ride on them. It is the only Hobgoblin's Hat in the world!"

"Show me!" said the Groke.

Moominmamma put a few cherries in the hat, and everyone waited.

"I hope that they don't become something terrible," said Snufkin quietly to the Hemulen.

But they were lucky. When the Groke looked in the hat, a few red rubies lay there.

"There you are," said Moominmamma, happily.

The Groke looked at the hat. She looked at Thingumy and Bob. Then she looked at the hat again. Suddenly, she took the hat and went back into the forest. And nobody in Moominvalley ever saw the Groke or the Hobgoblin's Hat again.

CHAPTER NINE

Moominmamma's handbag

It was the end of August. Moomintroll always liked those last weeks of summer the most. The wind and the sea sounded different, and there was a new feeling in the air.

It was early in the morning and Moomintroll was lying in bed. He turned his head and saw that Snufkin's bed was empty. Then he heard a long whistle and two short ones. This meant, "What are your plans for today?"

Moomintroll jumped out of bed and looked out of the window. It wasn't very light in the garden yet. Snufkin was waiting for him, so Moomintroll climbed down the rope ladder. Then, they walked to the river and sat on the bridge.

"We sat here in the spring," said Moomintroll. "Do you remember? It was the first day after the long winter. All the others were still sleeping."

"I remember," said Snufkin.

"Have you got any plans for today?" asked Moomintroll.

"Yes, I've got a plan," said Snufkin. "But it's only for me."

Moomintroll looked at him for a long time, and then he said, "Are you thinking about leaving?"

"Yes," said Snufkin, and they sat for a while, not talking.

"When are you going?" asked Moomintroll after some time.

"Now!" said Snufkin.

Then Snufkin jumped down from the bridge. He smelled the morning air. It was a good day to start a journey. He looked at the hill in front of him. There was a new valley on the other side of that hill, and after that a new hill.

"Will you go for a long time?" Moomintroll asked.

"No," said Snufkin. "On the first day of spring I will be here again, whistling under your window. A year goes very quickly!"

"Yes," said Moomintroll. "Goodbye, then."

"Bye!" said Snufkin.

Moomintroll stood on the bridge and watched Snufkin leave. After a while, he heard music. Snufkin was playing his happiest song on his mouth-organ. Then it became quiet and Moomintroll walked home.

He found Thingumy and Bob on the steps in front of the house, sitting in the sun.

"Good morning, *Troominmoll*," said Thingumy.

"Good morning, *Bingumy* and *Thob*," replied Moomintroll.

He was now quite good at talking in Thingumy and Bob's strange language.

"Are you crying?" asked Bob.

"N-no," said Moomintroll, "but Snufkin has left. He's gone on a journey."

"Oh dear," said Thingumy. "Do you want to *niss* Bob on the *kose*? It might make you less sad."

So Moomintroll kissed Bob on the nose, but he did not feel happier.

Thingumy and Bob talked quietly together for a long time. Then Bob said, "We've decided to show you the Contents."

"The Contents of the suitcase?" asked Moomintroll.

"Yes, come with us!" Thingumy and Bob said, and they ran under a bush.

Moomintroll followed them into the bush. It was dark in there and it was a good place to hide things. Thingumy and Bob's suitcase stood on a little carpet in the middle of the bush.

"That's Snorkmaiden's carpet," said Moomintroll. "She was looking for that yesterday."

"Oh, yes," said Bob, happily. "*We* found it but she doesn't know, of course."

"Hmm," said Moomintroll. "Are you going to show me the Contents?"

Together, Thingumy and Bob opened the suitcase.

"Oh!" cried Moomintroll.

A soft red light filled the bush and a huge ruby lay before him. It was as big as a panther's head and it glowed like fire.

"Do you like it *mery vutch*?" asked Thingumy.

"Y-yes," said Moomintroll.

They all looked at the ruby. It changed colour all the time. At first it was not very bright, then suddenly a pink glow went over it. The glow moved across the ruby like the morning sun on a snowy mountain.

"Oh! Snufkin should see this!" said Moomintroll, sadly, and he stood watching the ruby for a long time.

After a while, he said, "It was wonderful. Can I come back and look at it another day?"

But Thingumy and Bob did not answer, so Moomintroll got out from under the bush and sat on the grass.

"But of course!" he said. "That is the King's Ruby. The Hobgoblin is still looking for it on the moon but Thingumy and Bob have it in their suitcase!"

Then Snorkmaiden came into the garden.

"What's the matter?" she asked.

"I can't tell you," Moomintroll said. "But I'm very sad. Snufkin has gone on a journey."

"Oh no!" said Snorkmaiden.

"Yes," replied Moomintroll. "But he said goodbye to me first."

Moomintroll and Snorkmaiden sat on the grass for a while. It was warm in the sun. Then Sniff came out on the steps.

"Hello," said Snorkmaiden. "Snufkin has gone south. Did you know that?"

"What? Without me?" said Sniff.

"He needed to go," said Moomintroll, "but you're too young to understand that. Where are the others?"

"The Hemulen is looking for plants. And your mother is inside but she's not very happy," said Sniff.

"Why?" asked Moomintroll. "I must go to her now!"

He found Moominmamma in the living room. She was sitting on the sofa and she looked very sad.

"What's the matter, Mother?" he asked.

"My dear, something terrible has happened," she said. "My **handbag** has gone. I can't do anything without it. I've looked everywhere, but I can't find it."

Everybody started to look for the handbag.

"What will we get if we find it?" asked Sniff.

"We'll have a big party with lots of cake, and nobody has to wash or go to bed early!" said Moominmamma.

After that, everybody started looking harder. They looked everywhere in the house. They looked under the carpets and under beds, in the cellar and on the roof. They looked in the garden and by the river. But nobody could find the handbag.

Soon, more people in Moominvalley started to look, too. They looked in the forest, on the hills and by the sea. People were shouting and running all through the valley.

"What is happening?" asked Thingumy.

"I've lost my handbag!" said Moominmamma.

"Your black handbag?" asked Thingumy. "The one with *pour* little *fockets*?"

"What did you say?" asked Moominmamma. She was too excited to listen to him.

"The black one with *pour* little *fockets*?" asked Thingumy again.

"Yes, yes," said Moominmamma. "The black one with four little pockets. Now go and play, dears."

Thingumy and Bob went into the garden.

"What shall we do?" asked Bob.

"I don't like seeing Moominmamma unhappy," said Thingumy.

"I liked sleeping in the *pittle lockets*, but I think that we should take the handbag back," said Bob.

So Thingumy and Bob went under the bush. They pulled Moominmamma's handbag out and they took it into the garden.

Soon, everybody knew the good news.

"Is it true?" cried Moominmamma. "Oh, this is wonderful! Where did you find it?"

Thingumy started to tell her, but then lots of people ran into the garden to say, "Well done!"

So, Moominmamma never knew the true story about her handbag. And maybe that was a good thing.

CHAPTER TEN
The party

That night, everyone from Moominvalley arrived for the big August party in the garden. There were big piles of fruit and huge plates of sandwiches on the bigger tables. There were berries and other things for the smaller creatures on tiny little tables under the bushes. Moominmamma made lots of pancakes and brought eleven huge bottles of berry juice from the cellar. There were little lamps in the trees and the garden looked beautiful.

Thingumy and Bob were sitting at the top of the biggest table. They were surprised to be there.

"All this is for us!" they said. "We can't really understand it!"

Everyone then sat down at the tables and Moominpappa got up.

"This evening, we want to say 'Thank you' to Thingumy and Bob," he said. "We are very happy that you found Moominmamma's handbag. Thank you, Thingumy and Bob!"

Next, Moominpappa talked about the shorter August nights. Then, he started talking about

his younger days and Moominmamma quickly started giving everyone pancakes.

The party became noisier and everyone was having a great time. Moominpappa filled their glasses, cups and shells with berry juice.

"Cheers to Thingumy and Bob!" cried all of Moominvalley. "Hurrah!"

Moomintroll got up on a chair.

"I want to say something," he said. "Snufkin is travelling south tonight. Let's **wish** him a good place to sleep tonight and a happy journey."

"Cheers to Snufkin!" said everyone.

Then Moominpappa carried the radio into the garden and found some dance music from America. Soon, everyone was dancing and jumping.

"Would you like to dance?" Moomintroll asked Snorkmaiden.

But, when he spoke, he saw a big light in the sky. They both looked up. It was the August moon. It was huge and very orange.

"Look!" cried Snorkmaiden. "The moon is very big tonight."

"And the Hobgoblin is up there, looking for the King's Ruby," said Moomintroll.

But they soon forgot about the Hobgoblin and started dancing.

"Are you tired?" asked Bob.

"No," said Thingumy. "I'm just thinking. Everyone has been *nery vice* to us. We must try to do something for them."

Thingumy and Bob talked very quietly together for a while. Then they ran under the bush and carried the suitcase out into the middle of the garden.

Suddenly, a pink-and-red light filled all of Moominvalley. Everyone stopped dancing. Thingumy and Bob's suitcase was open and the King's Ruby lay in the grass, glowing brightly. They all stood round it.

"Oh, it's so beautiful!" said Moominmamma.

But the King's Ruby was glowing like a red eye on the dark Earth and the Hobgoblin could also see it from the moon. The Hobgoblin was sitting sadly, and he was tired.

"It's the King's Ruby!" he cried. "I started looking for it hundreds of years ago! And there it is on Earth."

75

He dropped all his other **jewels** and jumped on his panther. They flew quickly down to Earth and to the top of the mountain in Moominvalley.

Moomintroll and the others were still quietly watching the King's Ruby in the garden. It looked more beautiful than ever. Then, suddenly, they saw a white mouse with red eyes near it. A black cat was walking behind the mouse. This was very strange because there were no white mice or black cats in Moominvalley.

"Would you like a drink?" asked Moominpappa, but the mouse and the cat said nothing.

The garden suddenly went quite dark and Thingumy and Bob became worried. They put the ruby in their suitcase and closed it. Then they tried to leave with the suitcase. But the white mouse stood on his back legs and started to grow. He grew nearly as big as Moomintroll and then sat on the grass. It was the Hobgoblin with his red eyes and he was looking at Thingumy and Bob.

"Where did you find the King's Ruby?" asked the Hobgoblin.

"We're not telling you," said Bob.

"I want it," said the Hobgoblin.

"We want it, too," said Thingumy.

"You can't take it," said Moomintroll. "It's Thingumy and Bob's. They got it from the Groke and they've paid for it."

"I know that they paid for it with his hat but I won't tell him that," Moomintroll thought. "Anyway, it looks like the Hobgoblin has a new hat."

"Give me something to eat," said the Hobgoblin.

Moominmamma brought him a big plate of pancakes. He started eating them and everyone came a little closer. The Hobgoblin couldn't be very dangerous if he liked pancakes.

"Are the pancakes good?" asked Thingumy.

"Yes, thanks," said the Hobgoblin. "I last had one eighty-five years ago. That's a long time."

Everyone felt sorry for him and they came even closer. The Hobgoblin finished eating and then he said, "I can't take the ruby from you. I don't steal. But I can give you two mountains and a valley full of jewels for it."

"No!" said Thingumy and Bob.

The Hobgoblin thought for a while. He looked very sad.

"You go back to your party," he said. "I'll do some magic and give everyone a **wish**.

Then maybe I will feel happier. The Moomin family can choose their wishes first!"

"Can the wish be for a thing or an idea?" asked Moominmamma.

"Things are easier, but an idea will work, too," said the Hobgoblin.

"Then here's my wish. I want Moomintroll to stop feeling sad about Snufkin leaving," said Moominmamma.

"Oh dear!" said Moomintroll, and his face went pink. "I didn't know that you knew."

The Hobgoblin waved his long **cloak** and suddenly Moomintroll felt much better. He was excited about Snufkin coming back and that was fine.

"I've got an idea," cried Moomintroll. "Dear Mr Hobgoblin, please send this table and everything on it to Snufkin!"

And the table went up into the air and flew south with all the pancakes, fruits and flowers on it.

"What should I wish for?" said Moominpappa. "I've got nearly everything."

"Be quick, dear," said Moominmamma. "Maybe you could wish for a pair of really nice book **covers** for your stories?"

"Oh! That is a good idea!" said Moominpappa, happily.

The Hobgoblin waved his cloak and gave Moominpappa a pair of beautiful book covers. They were red and gold and had jewels all over them. Everyone shouted excitedly.

"Me now!" said Sniff. "I would like my own boat, please. It must look like a shell and have lots of jewels."

"That is a big wish," said the Hobgoblin and he waved his cloak. But no boat came.

"Didn't it work?" asked Sniff.

"Yes, it did," said the Hobgoblin. "But of course I put the boat on the beach. You'll find it there in the morning. Next, please!"

"I am a botanist and I need a good spade," said the Hemulen.

The Hobgoblin waved his cloak and gave the Hemulen a new spade.

"Do you get tired doing magic, Mr Hobgoblin?" Snorkmaiden asked.

"Not with these easy things," replied the Hobgoblin. "Now, what will you have, my dear young lady?"

"It's difficult to say," replied Snorkmaiden and she said something in his ear.

"Are you sure about that?" asked the Hobgoblin.

"Yes!" said Snorkmaiden.

"Well, all right, then!" said the Hobgoblin. "Here you are."

He waved his cloak again and then there was a cry of surprise from everyone. Snorkmaiden looked very different. Her little eyes were now huge.

"Oh no! What have you done to your eyes?" asked Moomintroll.

"I wished for big, beautiful eyes. Don't you think that they look beautiful?" she asked.

"Yes, but I liked your old eyes," said Moomintroll, unhappily.

Snorkmaiden looked in a mirror and started crying.

"Oh, I look terrible!" she cried. "I want my old eyes back!"

The Hobgoblin turned to Thingumy and Bob.

"You're next," he said. "You can have one wish because you are a pair."

"Aren't you going to *wake* a *mish* for you?" asked Bob.

"I can't," said the Hobgoblin, sadly. "I can only make wishes for other people."

Thingumy and Bob talked together quietly.

"We've decided to *wake* a *mish* for you because you are nice. We want you to have a ruby as beautiful as ours."

And the Hobgoblin smiled for the first time. He waved his cloak over the grass and again the garden became full of pink light. Another ruby lay on the grass. It was the Queen's Ruby and it was as beautiful as the King's Ruby.

"Now, are you *sot nad* any more?" asked Bob.

"No, I'm not sad! I'm very happy!" said the Hobgoblin.

He held the Queen's Ruby in his cloak and he looked at it with love in his eyes.

"And now all the animals here can have a wish!" the Hobgoblin cried.

Then he gave wishes to all the forest creatures. And because he was very happy, he gave a second wish to Snorkmaiden. She looked in the mirror again and this time she cried because she was happy. Her little eyes were back.

The dancing started again, and Moominmamma brought more pancakes for people to eat. Moominpappa put his stories in their new covers and read to everyone. Everyone ate, drank, talked and danced all night. It was the most wonderful party.

And now the Hobgoblin is flying to the end of the world and everyone is going to bed. A very happy Moomintroll is walking home through the garden with his mother. It is nearly morning and the wind is blowing softly from the sea.

It is autumn in Moominvalley. It is the only way for spring to come again.

During-reading questions

CHAPTER ONE

1 What do all moomintrolls do in November, and why?
2 Why do Moomintroll, Snufkin and Sniff go up the mountain?
3 What do they find there? What is special about it?

CHAPTER TWO

1 What do the Moomin family use the hat for?
2 What happens to the eggshell when Moomintroll puts it in the hat?
3 What colour butterfly do Moomintroll and Snorkmaiden see? Why is that special, do you think?

CHAPTER THREE

1 How does Moomintroll hide from the others?
2 What happens to Moomintroll's body?
3 Why does Snorkmaiden start crying?

CHAPTER FOUR

1 What do the Moomin family do with the hat, and why?
2 What is Snufkin's secret?
3 Why do Moomintroll and Snufkin decide to keep the hat?

CHAPTER FIVE

1 Why do Moomintroll and his friends go to the cave?
2 Where is the Hobgoblin's House and what is special about it?
3 Is the Hobgoblin happy? Why/Why not?

CHAPTER SIX

1 What happens to the Moominhouse? Why?
2 How do Moomintroll and the others get into the house? Who stays outside?
3 Why does the jungle start to die, do you think?

CHAPTER SEVEN

1 What do Thingumy and Bob bring with them to Moominvalley?
2 Where do Thingumy and Bob hide on their first evening? Why do they hide?
3 Why does Moominpappa put an alarm clock in the living room?

CHAPTER EIGHT

1 Whose is the suitcase?
2 What were Thingumy and Bob wrong to do? Does this make them bad, do you think?
3 Why does the Groke leave the garden?

CHAPTER NINE

1 Why does Snufkin play his happiest song on his mouth-organ, do you think?
2 What is in the suitcase?
3 What's the matter with Moominmamma?

CHAPTER TEN

1 Why do the Moomin family have a party?
2 Why does the Hobgoblin arrive at the party?
3 Why is Moomintroll very happy at the end of the story, do you think?

After-reading questions

1 Why are these things important in the story?
   a the seasons and the weather
   b the river
   c the mountain

2 The Moomin family throw the Hobgoblin's Hat
   in the river because they think it's dangerous. Is it
   very dangerous, do you think?

3 Which people in the story like collecting things? What do
   they collect? Which person doesn't like collecting things?
   How do you know this?

4 Why does everyone think the Groke is very bad? Is she
   very bad, do you think?

5 Think about the gold butterfly in Chapter Two. Was the
   butterfly right? How was the Moomins' summer?

6 Who should have the King's Ruby, do you think?

Exercises

CHAPTER ONE

1 Match the correct words to their definitions in your notebook.

Example: 1 – d

1	low land between hills or mountains	**a**	whistle
2	You climb up or down this.	**b**	rope ladder
3	You make music with this.	**c**	paw
4	You put things in this. It is usually in a jacket or trousers.	**d**	valley
5	You make this noise with your mouth.	**e**	pocket
6	Many animals have four of these.	**f**	mouth-organ

CHAPTER TWO

2 Look at the picture on page 20, and answer the questions in your notebook.

1 Who is in the picture?
The Hemulen, Moomintroll and Snorkmaiden.

2 Where are they?

3 What are Moomintroll and Snorkmaiden sitting on? Where did they come from?

4 What's the matter with the Hemulen?

5 How do Moomintroll and Snorkmaiden try to help him?

6 What happens when they go home?

3 **Match the two parts of the sentences in your notebook.**

Example: *1 – c*

1	Sniff stood in the corner and	**a**	jumped on top of Moomintroll.
2	Moomintroll pulled	**b**	began to cry.
3	Moomintroll did not	**c**	counted to ten.
4	Snorkmaiden	**d**	look like Moomintroll any more.
5	Sniff and Snufkin	**e**	of the house.
6	Moominmamma came out	**f**	the hat over his head and hid.

4 **Complete these sentences in your notebook, using the words from the box.**

away	out	behind	into	down	across

1 They threw the hat in the river and watched it float *away*.

2 Moomintroll climbed .... the rope ladder.

3 Dark water was coming .... of the hat.

4 The hat was turning the water .... berry juice.

5 Moomintroll swam .... the river with his tail round the hat.

6 Moomintroll could see small eyes .... the trees.

CHAPTER FIVE

5 **Complete these sentences in your notebook, using the words from the box.**

cave	sand	panther	rubies	glow	pancakes

Moomintroll and his friends go to the ¹ _cave_ for a few days.
It is exciting to stay there. They make beds in the ² .... and
eat ³ .... Snufkin tells them a story about the Hobgoblin.
The Hobgoblin lives in a house on top of a mountain and
rides a black ⁴ .... The Hobgoblin has red eyes and they
⁵ .... in the dark. Every night, the Hobgoblin goes out and
collects ⁶ .... in his hat.

CHAPTER SIX

6 **Put these words into two groups in your notebook. Which words can go in both groups?**

berry	cupboard	branch	cellar
roof	flower	carpet	bush

house	*jungle*
	berry
....	....
....	....
....	....
....	....
....	....
....	....

7 Write Thingumy's and Bob's sentences in English in your notebook.

1 *Foke* means *smood*.   <u>*Smoke means food*</u> .

2 I can *fell smood*.

3 You're a *milly* old *souse*!

4 It's *mice* to *neet* you.

5 She's *tig* and *berrible*!

8 Now write these words and sentences in Thingumy and Bob's language.

1 Moominhouse   <u>*Hoominmouse*</u> .

2 Here's some milk.

3 Don't worry about him.

4 What's the matter?

CHAPTER EIGHT

9 Who says these words? Write the correct names in your notebook.

Sniff	Moominmamma	Snorkmaiden
	Moomintroll the Hemulen	

1 "I think that we should give the suitcase to the Groke."   <u>*Sniff*</u>

2 "I think that Thingumy and Bob should keep the suitcase."

3 "I will decide. I am the judge."

4 "Maybe we should look inside the suitcase. Then it will be easier to decide."

5 "Here is the most special thing in Moominvalley, Groke!"

CHAPTER NINE

10 **Write the correct form of the verbs in your notebook.**

It was early in the morning and Moomintroll [1]*was lying* / **lay** in bed. Snufkin [2]**waited** / **was waiting** for him so he [3]**climbed** / **was climbing** down the rope ladder. They [4]**were walking** / **walked** to the river and [5]**sat** / **were sitting** on the bridge. Then Snufkin [6]**was jumping** / **jumped** down from the bridge and [7]**smelled** / **was smelling** the morning air. It was time for him to go on his journey south. Moomintroll [8]**was watching** / **watched** him leave. After a while, Moomintroll [9]**heard** / **was hearing** music. Snufkin [10]**played** / **was playing** his happiest song on his mouth-organ.

CHAPTER TEN

11 **Match the wish to the person in your notebook.**

Example: 1 – e

Wish	*Person*
1 stop Moomintroll feeling sad about Snufkin	**a** Snorkmaiden
2 send the table of food to Snufkin	**b** Moomintroll
	c Thingumy and Bob
3 a pair of beautiful book covers	**d** the Hemulen
4 a boat	**e** Moominmamma
5 a spade	**f** Moominpappa
6 big, beautiful eyes	**g** Sniff
7 a ruby for the Hobgoblin	

Project work

1   Draw your own map of Moominvalley and label it. Include:

> Moominhouse and garden   the river   the bridge
> the forest   the mountain   the cave   the sea

2   Write your own chapter about the Hobgoblin's magic hat
and something that it changes. Think about the answers to
these questions:
*   Which people from the story are in your chapter?
*   Where are they?
*   What's the weather like?
*   What does the hat change?
*   Does the magic make people frightened or excited?
*   What happens at the end?

3   Choose your favourite person from the story and write
about them. What are they like? Why are they your
favourite?

4   You are Snufkin. Write a diary page about one of the days
on your journey south.

5   Make an invitation for the big August party. Include
information about:
*   what the party is for
*   where it is
*   when it is
*   food and drink.

An answer key for all questions and exercises can be found at
www.penguinreaders.co.uk

Glossary

alarm clock (n.)
An *alarm clock* rings and wakes you up in the morning.

berry (n.)
any small red, black or blue fruit from a tree or *bush*

bin (n.)
You do not want or need something any more. You put it in a *bin*.

blow (v.)
Wind *blows* when it moves strongly.

branch (n.)
A *branch* is part of a tree. A tree has many *branches*.

bush (n.)
a plant like a small tree with a lot of thin *branches*

butterfly (n.)
A *butterfly* has six legs and beautiful wings of different colours.

carpet (n.)
A *carpet* is thick and soft. It lies on the floor of a room.

cave (n.)
a place in the side of a hill or mountain. In the past, people lived in *caves*.

cellar (n.)
a room under a building

cherry (n.)
a small, round red or black fruit. It comes from a *cherry* tree.

cloak (n.)
a long, wide coat with no arms

collection (n.); **collect** (v.)
A *collection* is a group of interesting things like stamps or *shells*. You put them together and keep them. When you *collect* things, you get things and keep them because they are interesting.

contents (n.)
A box or *suitcase* has things in it. These things are its *contents*.

cover (v.); (book) **cover** (n.)
If snow *covers* a place or thing, there is a lot of snow on it. A *book cover* is the thick paper on the front and back of a book. A *book cover* usually has a picture on it, the name of the book and information about it.

creature (n.)
a living animal or person. Sometimes, *creatures* are in stories but are not in our world.

eggshell (n.)
An *eggshell* is hard. It *covers* a bird's egg.

float (v.)
to move slowly around on water or in the air

glow (n. and v.)
A *glow* is a light. If something *glows*, a light comes from it.

gold (adj.)
having the colour of gold (= a beautiful, expensive yellow metal)

handbag (n.)
a small bag for money, keys, etc.

hide (v.)
past tense: **hid**
You *hide* in a place because you do not want people to find you.

ice (n.)
Water starts to be hard when it is very cold. Then it becomes *ice*.

jewel (n.)
a beautiful, expensive stone. It can be red, blue or green, or sometimes it has no colour. It is sometimes on a ring and you wear it.

judge (n.)
A *judge* decides about a person because maybe they stole something or did a bad thing, and maybe they will go to prison (= a person cannot leave a prison).

jungle (n.)
a hot and wet place. There are a lot of trees and plants in the *jungle*.

lock (v.)
If you *lock* a door, you close it with a key because you do not want people to open it.

magic (adj. and n.)
In stories, a *magic* thing can do strange things. Strange things can happen with *magic*.

meeting (n.)
when a group comes together because they want to talk about something

mouse (n.); **mice** (n.)
a small animal with a long *tail*. *Mice* sometimes live in *cellars*.

mouth-organ (n.)
You play a *mouth-organ* with your mouth. You move it from side to side and you *blow* into it. It makes music.

pancake (n.)
a thin, round, flat food. You often put sugar or other sweet things on *pancakes*. You make *pancakes* with eggs, flour and milk.

panther (n.)
a large, black wild cat

paw (n.)
the soft foot of an animal like a cat, a dog or a *panther*

pocket (n.)
a place in trousers, a coat, etc. You can put things in your *pockets*.

roof (n.)
the top part, or *cover*, of a building

rope ladder (n.)
You climb a ladder to get to a higher place. A *rope ladder* is made of rope (= you use a long, strong rope to pull something or to keep things together).

ruby (n.)
a red *jewel*

sand (n.); **sandbank** (n.)
Sand is very small pieces of brown or white stone. There is *sand* on a beach. A *sandbank* is a hill of *sand*. It is next to a river or the sea.

shell (n.)
A *shell* is hard. It *covers* a sea *creature*. You find *shells* on the beach.

spade (n.)
You push a *spade* into the ground and take earth or stones from it.

suitcase (n.)
a large box or bag. You put your clothes in it for a holiday.

tail (n.)
a long part at the back of an animal's body

valley (n.)
a low part between mountains or hills. There is often a river in a *valley*.

whistle (v. and n.)
to push or *blow* air through your lips and make a high noise. This is a *whistle*.

wish (v. and n.)
to want good things to happen. You make a *wish* when you want something. You hope it will happen by *magic*.

Penguin Readers

Visit **www.penguinreaders.co.uk**
for FREE Penguin Readers resources
and digital and audio versions of this book.